FoxSong

TORONTO   OXFORD   NEW YORK
OXFORD UNIVERSITY PRESS
1993

JOSEPH BRUCHAC

FoxSong

ILLUSTRATED BY
PAUL MORIN

Oxford University Press, 70 Wynford Drive, Don Mills, Ontario M3C 1J9

Toronto Oxford New York Delhi Bombay Calcutta Madras Karachi
Kuala Lumpur Singapore Hong Kong Tokyo Nairobi Dar es Salaam
Cape Town Melbourne Auckland Madrid
and associated companies in
Berlin Ibadan

Canadian Cataloguing in Publication Data
Bruchac, Joseph, 1942–
Fox song

ISBN 0–19–541000–9

1. Great-grandmothers – Juvenile fiction.
2. Indians of North America – Juvenile fiction.
3. Nature – Juvenile fiction.   4. Death – Juvenile fiction.
I. Morin, Paul, 1959–   II. Title.

PZ7.B783Fo 1993   j813'.54   C93–093475–X

Published in the United States by Philomel Books,
a division of The Putman & Grosset Group
200 Madison Ave., New York, NY 10016

1 2 3 4 — 6 5 4 3
Printed in Hong Kong

To the elders and the children — J.B.

To Nook, who helped me understand
the circle of life — P.M.

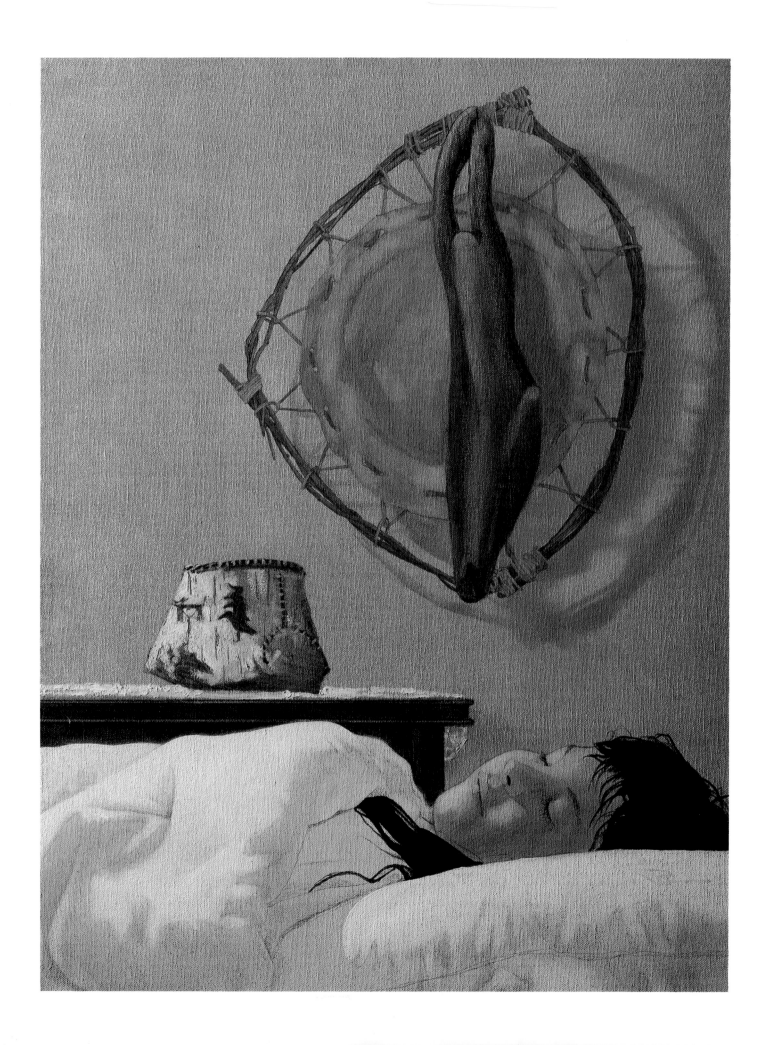

The sun came slanting in through the window at the foot of Jamie's bed. She felt it on her face, but she didn't want to open her eyes. She knew what she would have to remember when she opened her eyes. She felt so alone. Perhaps now if she kept her eyes closed, she might be able to find her way back into the dream where Grama Bowman was with her.

There were so many things that she and Grama Bowman did together. It had been that way ever since Jamie could remember. Grama Bowman was actually her great-grandmother. She was Abenaki Indian and the mother of Jamie's mother's mother, and she was over ninety years old when she came to live with them in their house on the Winooski

River, with the maple woods up the hill behind them. Such a long time ago, Jamie thought, six whole years. Most of my life. But not long enough. She kept her eyes closed, hearing Grama Bowman's voice telling her stories, seeing pictures in her mind of the things Grama Bowman and she loved to do together.

She saw them walking up Fox Hill in the heat of summer toward the slopes where the blackberries grew wild. Together they would pick out the berries that were, as Grama put it, "Just a little too ripe for us to take back, so we have to eat them here." Those berries were always the sweetest ones. Jamie remembered Grama explaining to her how their old people always cared for *alniminal,* the wild berries.

"They took care of them for hundreds of years before your father's people came here from France," Grama said. "Your father's people were good people. They learned from us that you have to burn off the dead bushes each year so that the new ones will be green and strong." Grama Bowman smiled. "His people were quick to learn, and we were ready to teach them. I think that is why we have kept on marrying them all these years." Jamie nodded and smiled, even though she was not quite sure what the joke was. She knew it was one of those things that Grama Bowman told her to hold on to and remember because the knowing of it would come to her when she was a little older.

The sun's warmth was even stronger on her face now.
Jamie heard her mother come into the room and stand by
the bed. Her shadow was cool across Jamie's face, but Jamie
lay still, knowing her mother would not bother her.

Her mother's soft steps went out of the room. Jamie looked
for another memory and found them walking along the river
until they came to the grove of birch trees. It was spring and
the trees were green with buds.

Grama Bowman put her hand on the trunk of one of the trees. "You see this mark here?" she said, pointing to the shape on the bark that looked almost like a bird. "We Abenaki say this is the mark of Badogi, the Thunder. The lightning is his arrow and he shoots it during the storms. But he doesn't want to hurt our people and so he marked these trees. Lightning never strikes these birch trees, so if you have to be near any tree in a storm, better to be near a young birch tree."

Jamie looked up and nodded. "I understand, Grama."

Grama Bowman took some tobacco from her pouch and placed it near the base of the tree. "Brother, we are going to take some of your clothing," she said to the tree. "We thank you for this piece of your blanket." Grama Bowman smiled at Jamie. "You know, that is our Indian name for the birch. We call it *maskwa*, blanket tree." She took her knife and made a cut straight down the bark.

"We don't take too much so the tree won't die, Grama?"

"That is the way, Granddaughter, our old Indian way. Be careful what we take and only take what we need. Now," she said, "you help me pull. We must go this way, to the left. The same direction the sun goes around the sky."

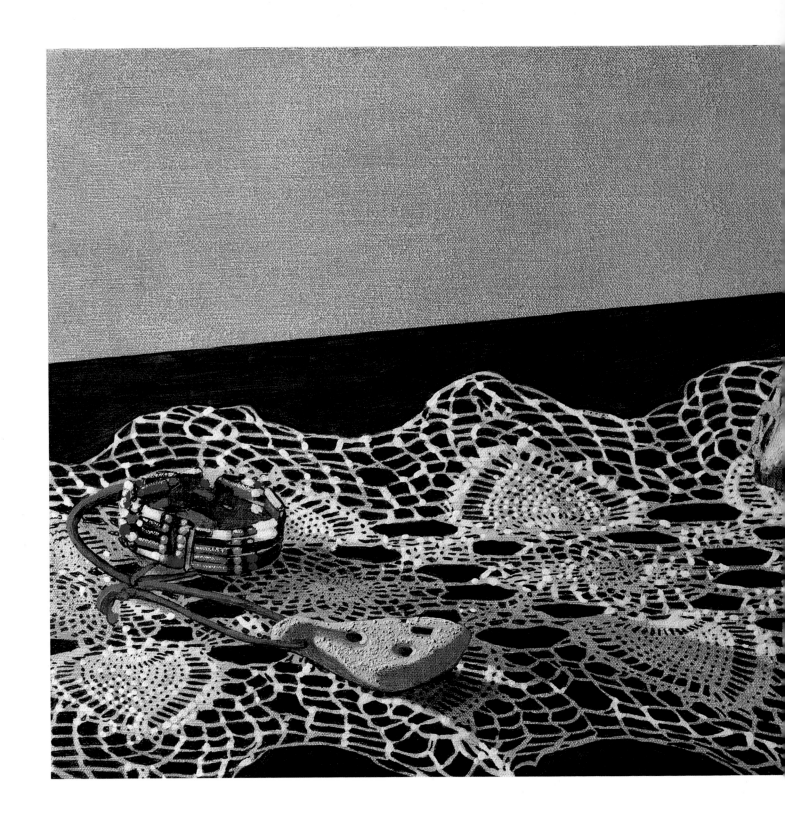

The basket they had made that day, using spruce roots to sew it together after folding it and making holes with Grama Bowman's bone awl, was sitting on Jamie's table near her bed. She opened her eyes for a moment to look at it, and she could still see the patterns on the basket that her grandmother

had made. The shapes of birds and ferns and animals. And her grandmother's bone awl was in that basket now. She hadn't understood why Grama Bowman had given it to her from her bag when she last saw her. Now she knew. She closed her eyes again, looking for her grandmother's face.

Grama Bowman's feet crunched through the snow in her white snow boots as they started on the trail to the maple grove up Fox Hill. Those boots were so big that the first time Jamie put them on—when she was a little girl—she couldn't move in them without falling. Grama Bowman always pretended that she couldn't remember which pair was hers and which was Jamie's. She would sit and struggle to put on Jamie's little galoshes while Jamie would stand in Grama's, giggling and saying, "Grama, I really think that these may be yours!" Finally they would have their galoshes on and they would finish the tea that Jamie's mother always insisted they drink before going out to check on the trees.

"Warm inside, warm outside," Jamie's mother said.

"You see, Granddaughter," Grama Bowman said, "that is the way the circle of life goes. You take care of your children when they are little ones and when you get old your children will take care of you. And they will tell you what to do, too!" The way she said it made everyone smile. Grama Bowman had a way of pursing up her face that would make her look like a little girl.

Then they went out into the late winter snow and up the trail toward the maple grove. All along the way Grama would point things out, the way the ice had formed on the twigs, the places where deer had browsed on the trees, the tracks of the animals. She loved to tell Jamie the stories those tracks told her. Listening to Grama's words, Jamie could see the animals as if they were still there.

"Old Owl, Kokohas, he dove down right there for Madegwas, the Rabbit," Grama said. "You see his wing marks on the snow? But Rabbit, he was too quick."

As they walked along, there was one set of tracks that Grama Bowman especially loved to see. "Look," she would say, "those are the prints of my best friend, Wokwses, the Fox. She is a clever one. I know her tracks well. Now she is out looking for her old man. She wants to have some little ones for the spring. Sometime," Grama Bowman said, "when you are out here and I am not with you, you keep your eyes open. You might see her and when you do, you will think of me."

Jamie nodded but she wasn't sure that she understood. She couldn't imagine being in the woods without Grama by her side.

It was another quarter of a mile beyond that clearing where they saw the tracks of the fox that they came to the line of trees that Jamie's father tapped for maple syrup. He would be along later in the morning with his tractor to collect the sap, but Grama always insisted that it was important for the two of them to come out whenever they could, just to make sure things were going right.

"We have to taste this sap and see that it is good," Grama Bowman said. She unhooked one of the buckets and tilted it so that Jamie could drink. There was nothing as light and subtly sweet as that taste.

Jamie opened her eyes and blinked away the tears. She closed her eyes again, afraid that she would no longer be able to see her grandmother in her memory.

But instead she found herself walking beside her along the hillslope. It was autumn, the leaves blowing in the wind, and it was very early in the morning. The sun was just coming up.

"My old Indian people," Grama Bowman said, "told me that the leaves love to dance. But they can only do their best dancing when they are ready to give themselves to the wind. That is when they are old, but they are the most beautiful then. They put on their best colors and then they dance."

A leaf came drifting past them and it brushed Jamie's face. It spiraled in the wind, went up and down, and then it touched the earth.

"When I see the leaves," Grama Bowman said, "I see my old people and remember they are still with me. We say that those who have gone are no further away from us than the leaves that have fallen."

The sun was a red arc lifting over the ridge and Grama reached out for Jamie's hand. "I brought you here to teach you a song. I forgot to teach it to my own daughter. But I know that you'll remember this song. It is a welcoming song and it says hello to the new day. It says hello to every new person you meet and it welcomes them. When you sing it, you will not be alone."

Grama Bowman began to tap her open palm on her leg as they sat there in the fallen leaves, facing the east. In a clear high voice she sang:

Hey, kwah nu deh
Hey, kwah nu deh, kwah nu deh
Hey, kwah nu deh
Hey, kwah nu deh, kwah nu deh
Hey, hey, kwah nu deh

She sang it twice and the second time she sang it, Jamie sang with her. By the time they finished, the sun was up and its warmth was on their faces.

Jamie opened her eyes and sat up. She felt the sun on her face and she got out of bed. She hadn't taken her clothes off from the night before, and her mother had come in and covered her as she lay on the bed. She went out of her room, past her grandmother's empty room. She went downstairs and walked through the kitchen. Her mother and father were there, but they said nothing to her. She loved them for that understanding. She took her light jacket from its peg near the back door and went outside.

As soon as she reached the path she began to run, her feet scattering the leaves that gleamed yellow and red in the October morning light. When she reached the slope that looked over their house toward the east, she leaned back against the same tree where Grama Bowman used to sit, and faced the sun. She took four deep breaths and the racing of her heart slowed. Then, still facing the sun, she began to sing:

Hey, kwah nu deh
Hey, kwah nu deh, kwah nu deh

Something moved at the edge of her vision and she turned her head slowly. A meadowlark came flying out of the bushes at the edge of the clearing. Then, a few steps behind it, a small dog came walking out. It stood perfectly still. Jamie saw it wasn't a dog at all, it was a fox. It was as if it was waiting for something. Jamie began to sing again:

Hey, kwah nu deh
Hey, kwah nu deh, kwah nu deh
Hey, kwah nu deh

The fox yawned and sat down on its haunches. The sunlight was bright on its coat and its eyes glistened. Jamie continued the song:

Hey, kwah nu deh
Hey, kwah nu deh, kwah nu deh
Hey, kwah nu deh
Hey, kwah nu deh, kwah nu deh
Hey, hey, kwah nu deh

Jamie finished the song and looked away from the fox. She closed her eyes, feeling the warmth of the sun, which touched her face and touched the earth. When she opened her eyes again, the fox was gone. Had it really been there? She didn't know, but as she rose and went back down the hill, she knew that she would never be alone.

A NOTE ABOUT THIS STORY

In many ways, *Fox Song* is a family story. My grandmother had a pet fox when she was a girl, and I grew up hearing stories about it. I still live in the house in which my grandparents raised me. So, as I walk in the woods by our home I often think about that story and other stories I was told about animals by my grandparents. The tradition of grandparents and great-grandparents living with the family is still common among the Abenaki people.

One of my friends and teachers was a Native elder named Swift Eagle. Near the end of his life, he told me I should always keep my eyes open for a little red fox and think of him when I saw it. A few months after his death, I was walking in the woods when a fox came right up to me and sat down as if waiting for something. I sang it a song that Swift Eagle had taught me. It listened, there in the autumn sunlight.

The song in *Fox Song* is not that song—which was a personal gift to me from Swift Eagle. Instead, I used an old Abenaki greeting song, one sung by one group of Abenaki people after being welcomed by another.